"Speaking of Operations—"

GARDEN CITY   NEW YORK
DOUBLEDAY, DORAN & COMPANY, Inc.

APPARENTLY THERE WAS NOBODY
AT HOME

"Speaking of Operations—"

By
Irvin S. Cobb

Author of
"Back Home," "Europe Revised," Etc., Etc.

Illustrations by TONY SARG

Garden City   New York

Doubleday, Doran & Company, Inc.

"Speaking of Operations—"

RESPECTFULLY DEDICATED
TO TWO CLASSES:

THOSE WHO HAVE ALREADY BEEN OPERATED ON

THOSE WHO HAVE NOT YET BEEN OPERATED ON

"Speaking of Operations—"

CONTENTS

Mainly My Own

"*Speaking of Operations—*"

ILLUSTRATIONS

NOW that the last belated bill for services professionally rendered has been properly paid and properly receipted; now that the memory of the event, like the mark of the stitches, has faded out from a vivid red to a becoming pink shade; now that I pass a display of adhesive tape in a drug-store window without flinching—I sit me down to write a little piece about a certain matter—a small thing, but mine own—to wit, That Operation.

For years I have noticed that persons who underwent pruning or remodeling at the hands of a duly qualified surgeon, and survived, like to talk about it afterward. In the event of their not surviving I have no doubt they still liked to talk about it, but in a different locality. Of all the readily available topics for use, whether among friends or among strangers, an operation seems to be the handiest and most dependable. It beats the Tariff, or Roosevelt, or Bryan, or when this war is going to end, if ever, if you are a man talking to other men; and it is more exciting even than the question of how Mrs. Vernon Castle will wear her hair this season, if you are a woman talking to other women.

For mixed companies a whale is one of the best and the easiest things to talk about that I know of. In regard to whales and their peculiarities you can make almost any assertion without fear of successful contradiction. Nobody ever knows any more about them than you do. You are not hampered by facts. If someone mentions the blubber of the whale and you chime in and say it may be noticed for miles on a still day when the large but emotional creature has been moved to tears by some great sorrow coming into its life, everybody is bound to accept the statement. For after all how few among us really know whether a distressed whale sobs aloud or does so under its breath? Who, with any certainty, can tell whether a mother whale hatches her own egg her own self or leaves it on the sheltered bosom of a fjord to be incubated by the gentle warmth of the midnight sun? The possibilities of the proposition for purposes of informal debate, pro and con, are apparent at a glance.

The weather, of course, helps out amazingly when you are meeting people for the first time, because there is nearly always more or less weather going on somewhere and practically everybody has ideas about it. The human breakfast is also a wonderfully good topic to start up during one of those lulls. Try it yourself the next time the conversation seems to drag. Just speak up in an offhand kind of way and say that you never care much about breakfast—a slice of toast and a cup of weak tea start you off properly for doing a hard day's work. You will be surprised to note how things liven up and how eagerly all present join in. The lady on your left feels that you should know she always takes two lumps of sugar and nearly half cream, because she simply cannot abide hot milk, no matter what the doctors say. The gentleman on your right will be moved to confess he likes his eggs boiled for exactly three minutes, no more and no less. Buckwheat cakes and sausage find a champion and oatmeal rarely lacks a warm defender.

But after all, when all is said and done, the king of all topics is operations. Sooner or later, wherever two or more are gathered together it is reasonably certain that somebody will bring up an operation.

Until I passed through the experience of being operated on myself, I never really realized what a precious conversational boon the subject is, and how great a part it plays in our intercourse with our fellow beings on this planet. To the teller it is enormously interesting, for he is not only the hero of the tale but the rest of the cast and the stage setting as well—the whole show, as they say; and if the listener has had a similar experience—and who is there among us in these days that has not taken a nap 'neath the shade of the old ether cone?—it acquires a doubled value.

"Speaking of operations ——" you say, just like that, even though nobody present has spoken of them; and then you are off, with your new acquaintance sitting on the edge of his chair, or hers as the case may be and so frequently is, with hands clutched in polite but painful restraint, gills working up and down with impatience, eyes brightened with desire, tongue hung in the middle, waiting for you to pause to catch your breath, so that he or she may break in with a few personal recollections along the same line. From a mere conversation it resolves itself into a symptom symposium, and a perfectly splendid time is had by all.

If an operation is such a good thing to talk about, why isn't it a good thing to write about, too? That is what I wish to know. Besides, I need the money. Verily, one always needs the money when one has but recently escaped from the ministering clutches of the modern hospital. Therefore I write.

It all dates back to the fair, bright morning when I went to call on a prominent practitioner here in New York, whom I shall denominate as Doctor X. I had a pain. I had had it for days. It was not a dependable, locatable pain, such as a tummyache or a toothache is, which you can put your hand on; but an indefinite, unsettled, undecided kind of pain, which went wandering about from place to place inside of me like a strange ghost lost in Cudjo's Cave. I never knew until then what the personal sensations of a haunted house are. If only the measly thing could have made up its mind to settle down somewhere and start light housekeeping I think I should have been better satisfied. I never had such an uneasy tenant. Alongside of it a woman with the moving fever would be comparatively a fixed and stationary object.

Having always, therefore, enjoyed perfectly riotous and absolutely unbridled health, never feeling weak and distressed unless dinner happened to be ten or fifteen minutes late, I was green regarding physicians and the ways of physicians. But I knew Doctor X slightly, having met him last summer in one of his hours of ease in the grand stand at a ball game, when he was expressing a desire to cut the umpire's throat from ear to ear, free of charge; and I remembered his name, and remembered, too, that he had impressed me at the time as being a person of character and decision and scholarly attainments.

He wore whiskers. Somehow in my mind whiskers are ever associated with medical skill. I presume this is a heritage of my youth, though I believe others labor under the same impression. As I look back it seems to me that in childhood's days all the doctors in our town wore whiskers.

I recall one old doctor down there in Kentucky who was practically lurking in ambush all the time. All he needed was a few decoys out in front of him and a pump gun to be a duck blind. He carried his calomel about with him in a fruit jar, and when there was a cutting job he stropped his scalpel on his bootleg.

You see, in those primitive times germs had not been invented yet, and so he did not have to take any steps to avoid them. Now we know that loose, luxuriant whiskers are unsanitary, because they make such fine winter quarters for germs; so, though the doctors still wear whiskers, they do not wear them wild and waving. In the profession bosky whiskers are taboo; they must be landscaped. And since it is a recognized fact that germs abhor orderliness and straight lines they now go elsewhere to reside, and the doctor may still retain his traditional aspect and yet be practically germproof. Doctor X was trimmed in accordance with the ethics of the newer school. He had trellis whiskers. So I went to see him at his offices in a fashionable district, on an expensive side street.

Before reaching him I passed through the hands of a maid and a nurse, each of whom spoke to me in a low, sorrowful tone of voice, which seemed to indicate that there was very little hope.

I reached an inner room where Doctor X was. He looked me over, while I described for him as best I could what seemed to be the matter with me, and asked me a number of intimate questions touching on the lives, works, characters and peculiarities of my ancestors; after which he made me stand up in front of him and take my coat off, and he punched me hither and yon with his forefinger. He also knocked repeatedly on my breastbone with his

[18]

knuckles, and each time, on doing this, would apply his ear to my chest and listen intently for a spell, afterward shaking his head in a disappointed way. Apparently there was nobody at home. For quite a time he kept on knocking, but without getting any response.

He then took my temperature and fifteen dollars, and said it was an interesting case —not unusual exactly, but interesting—and that it called for an operation.

From the way my heart and other organs jumped inside of me at that statement I knew at once that, no matter what he may have thought, the premises were not unoccupied. Naturally I inquired how soon he meant to operate. Personally I trusted there was no hurry about it. I was perfectly willing to wait for several years, if necessary. He smiled at my ignorance.

"I never operate," he said; "operating is entirely out of my line. I am a diagnostician."

He was, too—I give him full credit for that. He was a good, keen, close diagnostician. How did he know I had only fifteen dollars on me? You did not have to tell this man what you had, or how much. He knew without being told.

I asked whether he was acquainted with Doctor Y—Y being a person whom I had met casually at a club to which I belong. Oh, yes, he said, he knew Doctor Y. Y was a clever man, X said—very, very clever; but Y specialized in the eyes, the ears, the nose and the throat. I gathered from what Doctor X said that any time Doctor Y ventured below the thorax he was out of bounds and liable to be penalized; and that if by any chance he strayed down as far as the lungs he would call for help and back out as rapidly as possible.

This was news to me. It would appear that these up-to-date practitioners just go ahead and divide you up and partition you out among themselves without saying anything to you about it. Your torso belongs to one man and your legs are the exclusive property of his brother practitioner down on the next block, and so on. You may belong to as many as half a dozen specialists, most of whom, very possibly, are total strangers to you, and yet never know a thing about it yourself.

It has rather the air of trespass—nay, more than that, it bears some of the aspects of unlawful entry—but I suppose it is legal. Certainly, judging by what I am able to learn, the system is being carried on generally. So it must be ethical.

Anything doctors do in a mass is ethical. Almost anything they do singly and on individual responsibility is unethical. Being ethical among doctors is practically the same thing as being a Democrat in Texas or a Presbyterian in Scotland.

"Y will never do for you," said Doctor X, when I had rallied somewhat from the shock of these disclosures. "I would suggest that you go to Doctor Z, at such-and-such an address. You are exactly in Z's line. I'll let him know that you are coming and when, and I'll send him down my diagnosis."

So that same afternoon, the appointment having been made by telephone, I went, full of quavery emotions, to Doctor Z's place. As soon as I was inside his outer hallway

I realized that I was nearing the presence of one highly distinguished in his profession.

A pussy-footed male attendant, in a livery that made him look like a cross between a headwater and an undertaker's assistant, escorted me through an anteroom into a reception-room, where a considerable number of well-dressed men and women were sitting about in strained attitudes, pretending to read magazines while they waited their turns, but in reality furtively watching one another.

I sat down in a convenient chair, adhering fast to my hat and my umbrella. They were the only friends I had there and I was determined not to lose them without a struggle. On the wall were many colored charts showing various portions of the human anatomy and what ailed them. Directly in front of me was a very thrilling illustration, evidently copied from an oil painting, of a liver in a bad state of repair. I said to myself that if I had a liver like that one I should keep it hidden from the public eye—I would never permit it to sit

HE REGARDED IT AS A SUIT OF CLOTHES
BUT I KNEW BETTER

for its portrait. Still, there is no account-
ing for tastes. I know a man who got his
spleen back from the doctors and now keeps
it in a bottle of alcohol on the what-not in
the parlor, as one of his most treasured
possessions, and sometimes shows it to visi-
tors. He, however, is of a very saving
disposition.

Presently a lady secretary, who sat behind a roll-top desk in a corner of the room,
lifted a forefinger and silently beckoned me
to her side. I moved over and sat down
by her; she took down my name and my
age and my weight and my height, and a
number of other interesting facts that will
come in very handy should anyone ever be
moved to write a complete history of my
early life. In common with Doctor X she
shared one attribute—she manifested a
deep curiosity regarding my forefathers—
wanted to know all about them. I felt that
this was carrying the thing too far. I felt
like saying to her:

"Miss or madam, so far as I know there
is nothing the matter with my ancestors of
the second and third generations back, ex-

cept that they are dead. I am not here to seek medical assistance for a grandparent who succumbed to diasppointment that time when Samuel J. Tilden got counted out, or for a great-grandparent who entered into Eternal Rest very unexpectedly and in a manner entirely uncalled for as a result of being an innocent bystander in one of those feuds that were so popular in my native state immediately following the Mexican War. Leave my ancestors alone. There is no need of your shaking my family tree in the belief that a few overripe patients will fall out. I alone—I, me, myself —am the present candidate!"

However, I refrained from making this protest audibly. I judged she was only going according to the ritual; and as she had a printed card, with blanks in it ready to be filled out with details regarding the remote members of the family connection, I humored her along.

When I could not remember something she wished to know concerning an ancestor I supplied her with thrilling details culled from the field of fancy. When the card was entirely filled up she sent me back to my old place to wait. I waited and waited, breeding fresh ailments all the time. I had started out with one symptom; now if I had one I had a million and a half. I could feel goose flesh sprouting out all over me. If I had been taller I might have had more, but not otherwise. Such is the power of the human imagination when the surroundings are favorable to its development.

Time passed; to me it appeared that nearly all the time there was passed and that we were getting along toward the shank-end of the Christian era mighty fast. I was afraid my turn would come next and afraid it would not. Perhaps you know this sensation. You get it at the dentist's, and when you are on the list of after-dinner speakers at a large banquet, and when you are waiting for the father of the Only Girl in the World to make up his mind whether he is willing to try to endure you as a son-in-law.

Then some more time passed.

One by one my companions, obeying a

command, passed out through the door at the back, vanishing out of my life forever. None of them returned. I was vaguely wondering whether Doctor Z buried his dead on the premises or had them removed by a secret passageway in the rear, when a young woman in a nurse's costume tapped me on the shoulder from behind.

I jumped. She hid a compassionate smile with her hand and told me that the doctor would see me now.

As I rose to follow her—still clinging with the drowning man's grip of desperation to my hat and my umbrella—I was astonished to note by a glance at the calendar on the wall that this was still the present date. I thought it would be Thursday of next week at the very least.

Doctor Z also wore whiskers, carefully pointed up by an expert hedge trimmer. He sat at his desk, surrounded by freewill offerings from grateful patients and by glass cases containing other things he had taken away from them when they were not in a condition to object. I had expected, after all the preliminary ceremonies and delays, that we should have a long séance together. Not so; not at all. The modern expert in surgery charges as much for remembering your name between visits as the family doctor used to expect for staying up all night with you, but he does not waste any time when you are in his presence.

I was about to find that out. And a little later on I was to find out a lot of other things; in fact, that whole week was of immense educational value to me.

I presume it was because he stood so high in his profession, and was almost constantly engaged in going into the best society that Doctor Z did not appear to be the least bit excited over my having picked him out to look into me. In the most perfunctory manner he shook the hand that has shaken the hands of Jess Willard, George M. Cohan and Henry Ford, and bade me be seated in a chair which was drawn up in a strong light, where he might gaze directly at me as we conversed and so get the full values of the composition, But if I was a treat for him to look at he concealed his feelings very effectually.

He certainly had his emotions under splendid control. But then, of course, you must remember that he probably had traveled about extensively and was used to sight-seeing.

From this point on everything passed off in a most businesslike manner. He reached into a filing cabinet and took out an exhibit, which I recognized as the same one his secretary had filled out in the early part of the century. So I was already in the card-index class. Then briefly he looked over the manifest that Doctor X had sent him. It may not have been a manifest—it may have been an invoice or a bill of lading. Anyhow, I was in the assignee's hands. I could only hope it would not eventually become necessary to call in a receiver. Then he spoke:

"Yes, yes-yes," he said; "yes-yes-yes! Operation required. Small matter—hum, hum! Let's see—this is Tuesday? Quite so. Do it Friday! Friday at"—he glanced toward a scribbled pad of engagement dates at his elbow—"Friday at seven A. M.

No; make it seven-fifteen. Have important tumor case at seven. St. Germicide's
Hospital. You know the place?—up on
Umpty-umph Street. Go' day! Miss Who-
ziz, call next visitor."

And before I realized that practically
the whole affair had been settled I was
outside the consultation-room in a small
private hall, and the secretary was telling
me further details would be conveyed to
me by mail. I went home in a dazed state.
For the first time I was beginning to learn
something about an industry in which here-
tofore I had never been interested. Especially was I struck by the difference now
revealed to me in the preliminary stages of
the surgeons' business as compared with
their fellow experts in the allied cutting
trades—tailors, for instance, not to mention
barbers. Every barber, you know, used to
be a surgeon, only he spelled it chirurgeon.
Since then the two professions have drifted
far apart. Even a half-witted barber—the
kind who always has the first chair as you
come into the shop—can easily spend ten
minutes of your time thinking of things he

thinks you should have and mentioning them to you one by one, whereas any good, live surgeon knows what you have almost instantly.

As for the tailor—consider how wearisome are his methods when you parallel them alongside the tremendous advances in this direction made by the surgeon—how cumbersome and old-fashioned and tedious! Why, an experienced surgeon has you all apart in half the time the tailor takes up in deciding whether the vest shall fasten with five buttons or six. Our own domestic tailors are bad enough in this regard and the Old World tailors are even worse.

I remember a German tailor in Aix-la-Chapelle in the fall of 1914 who undertook to build for me a suit suitable for visiting the battle lines informally. He was the most literary tailor I ever met anywhere. He would drape the material over my person and then take a piece of chalk and write quite a nice long piece on me. Then he would rub it out and write it all over again, but more fully. He kept this up at intervals of every other day until he had writer's cramp. After that he used pins. He would pin the seams together, uttering little soothing, clucking sounds in German whenever a pin went through the goods and into me. The German cluck is not so soothing as the cluck of the English-speaking peoples, I find.

At the end of two long and trying weeks, which wore both of us down noticeably, he had the job done. It was not an unquali-fied success. He regarded it as a suit of clothes, but I knew better; it was a set of slip covers, and if only I had been a two-seated runabout it would have proved a perfect fit, I am sure; but I am a single-seated design and it did not answer. I wore it to the war because I had nothing else to wear that would stamp me as a regular war correspondent, except, of course, my wrist watch; but I shall not wear it to another war. War is terrible enough already; and, besides, I have parted with it. On my way home through Hol-land I gave that suit to a couple of poor Belgian refugees, and I presume they are still wearing it.

So far as I have been able to observe, the surgeons and the tailors of these times share but one common instinct: If you go to a new surgeon or to a new tailor he is morally certain, after looking you over, that the last surgeon you had, or the last tailor, did not do your cutting properly. There, however, is where the resemblance ends. The tailor, as I remarked in effect just now, wants an hour at least in which to decide how he may best cover up and disguise the irregularities of the human form; in much less time than that the surgeon has completely altered the form itself.

With the surgeon it is very much as it is with those learned men who write those large, impressive works of reference which should be permanently in every library, and which we are forever buying from an agent because we are so passionately addicted to payments. If the thing he seeks does not appear in the contents proper he knows exactly where to look for it. "See appendix," says the historian to you in a footnote. "See appendix," says the surgeon to himself, the while humming a cheery refrain. And so he does.

Well, I went home. This was Tuesday and the operation was not to be performed until the coming Friday. By Wednesday I had calmed down considerably. By Thursday morning I was practically normal again as regards my nerves. You will understand that I was still in a state of blissful ignorance concerning the actual methods of the surgical profession as exemplified by its leading exponents of today. The knowledge I have touched on in the pages immediately preceding was to come to me later.

Likewise Doctor Z's manner had been deceiving. It could not be that he meant to carve me to any really noticeable extent —his attitude had been entirely too casual. At our house carving is a very serious matter. Any time I take the head of the table and start in to carve it is fitting to remove the women and children to a place of safety, and onlookers should get under the table. When we first began housekeeping and gave our first small dinner-party we had a brace of ducks cooked in honor of the company, and I, as host, undertook to carve them. I never knew until then that a duck was built like a watch—that his works were inclosed in a burglarproof case. Without the use of dynamite the Red Leary-O'Brien gang could not have broken into those ducks. I thought so then and I think so yet. Years have passed since then, but I may state that even now, when there are guests for dinner, we do not have ducks. Unless somebody else is going to carve, we have liver.

I mention this fact in passing because it shows that I had learned to revere carving as one of the higher arts, and one not to be approached except in a spirit of due appreciation of the magnitude of the undertaking, and after proper consideration and thought and reflection, and all that sort of thing.

If this were true as regards a mere duck, why not all the more so as regards the carving of a person of whom I am so very fond as I am of myself? Thus I reasoned. And finally, had not Doctor Z spoken of the coming operation as a small matter? Well then?

Thursday at noon I received from Doctor Z's secretary a note stating that arrangements had been made for my admission into St. Germicide that same evening and that I was to spend the night there. This hardly seemed necessary. Still, the tone of the note appeared to indicate that the hospital authorities particularly wished to have me for an overnight guest; and as I reflected that probably the poor things had few enough bright spots in their busy lives, I decided I would humor them along and gladden the occasion with my presence from dinner-time on.

About eight o'clock I strolled in very jauntily. In my mind I had the whole programme mapped out. I would stay at the hospital for, say, two days following the operation—or, at most, three. Then I must be up and away. I had a good deal of work to do and a number of people to see on important business, and I could not really afford to waste more than a week-end on the staff of St. Germicide's. After Monday they must look to their own devices for social entertainment. That was my idea. Now when I look back on it I laugh, but it is a hollow laugh and there is no real merriment in it.

Indeed, almost from the moment of my entrance little things began to come up that were calculated to have a depressing effect on one's spirits. Downstairs a serious-looking lady met me and entered in a book a number of salient facts regarding my personality which the previous investigators had somehow overlooked. There is a lot of bookkeeping about an operation. This detail attended to, a young man, dressed in white garments and wearing an expression that stamped him as one who had suffered a recent deep bereavement, came and relieved me of my hand bag and escorted me upstairs.

As we passed through the upper corridors I had my first introduction to the hospital smell, which is a smell compounded of iodoform, ether, gruel, and something boiling. All hospitals have it,

IN WHICH I ASSUMED ALL RESPONSIBILITY
FOR WHAT WAS TO TAKE PLACE

I understand. In time you get used to it, but you never really care for it.

The young man led me into a small room tastefully decorated with four walls, a floor, a ceiling, a window sill and a window, a door and a doorsill, and a bed and a chair. He told me to go to bed. I did not want to go to bed—it was not my regular bed-time—but he made a point of it, and I judged it was according to regulations; so I undressed and put on my night clothes and crawled in. He left me, taking my other clothes and my shoes with him, but I was not allowed to get lonely.

A little later a ward surgeon appeared, to put a few inquiries of a pointed and personal nature. He particularly desired to know what my trouble was. I explained to him that I couldn't tell him—he would have to see Doctor X or Doctor Z; they probably knew, but were keeping it a secret between themselves.

The answer apparently satisfied him, because immediately after that he made me sign a paper in which I assumed all responsibility for what was to take place the next morning.

This did not seem exactly fair. As I pointed out to him, it was the surgeon's affair, not mine; and if the surgeon made a mistake the joke would be on him and not on me, because in that case I would not be here anyhow. But I signed, as requested, on the dotted line, and he departed.

After that, at intervals, the chief house surgeon dropped in, without knocking, and the head nurse came, and an interne or so, and a ward nurse, and the special nurse who was to have direct charge of me. It dawned on me that I was not having any more privacy in that hospital than a goldfish.

About eleven o'clock an orderly came, and, without consulting my wishes in the matter, he undressed me until I could have passed almost anywhere for September Morn's father, and gave me a clean shave, twice over, on one of my most prominent plane surfaces. I must confess I enjoyed that part of it. So far as I am able to recall, it was the only shave I have ever had where the operator did not spray me with cheap perfumery afterward and then try to sell me a bottle of hair tonic.

Having shaved me, the young man did me up amidships in a neat cloth parcel, took his kit under his arm and went away.

It occurred to me that, considering the trivial nature of the case, a good deal of fuss was being made over me by persons who could have no personal concern in the matter whatsoever. This thought recurred to me frequently as I lay there, all tied in a bundle like a week's washing. I did not feel quite so uppish as I had felt. Why was everybody picking on me?

Anon I slept, but dreamed fitfully. I dreamed that a whole flock of surgeons came to my bedside and charted me out in sections, like one of those diagram pictures you see of a beef in the Handy Compendium of Universal Knowledge, showing the various cuts and the butcher's pet name for each cut. Each man took his favorite joint and carried it away, and when they were all gone I was merely a recent site, full of reverberating echoes and nothing else.

I have had happier dreams in my time; this was not the kind of dream I should have selected had the choice been left to me.

When I woke the young sun was shining in at the window, and an orderly—not the orderly who had shaved me, but another one—was there in my room and my nurse was waiting outside the door. The orderly dressed me in a quaint suit of pyjamas cut on the half shell and buttoning stylishly in the back, *princesse mode*. Then he rolled in a flat litter on wheels and stretched me on it, and covered me up with a white table-cloth, just as though I had been cold Sunday-night supper, and we started for the operating-room at the top of the building; but before we started I lit a large black cigar, as Gen. U. S. Grant used to do when he went into battle. I wished by this to show how indifferent I was. Maybe he fooled somebody, but I do not believe I possess the same powers of simulation that Grant had. He must have been a very remarkable man—Grant must.

The orderly and the nurse trundled me

out into the hall and loaded me into an elevator, which was to carry us up to the top of the hospital. Several other nurses were already in the elevator. As we came aboard one of them remarked that it was a fine day. A fine day for what? She did not finish the sentence.

Everybody wore a serious look. Inside of myself I felt pretty serious too—serious enough for ten or twelve. I had meant to fling off several very bright, spontaneous quips on the way to the table. I thought them out in advance, but now, somehow, none of them seemed appropriate. Instinctively, as it were, I felt that humor was out of place here.

I never knew an elevator to progress from the third floor of a building to the ninth with such celerity as this one on which we were traveling progressed. Personally I was in no mood for haste. If there was anyone else in all that great hospital who was in a particular hurry to be operated on I was perfectly willing to wait. But alas, no! The mechanism of the elevator was in perfect order—entirely too perfect. No accident of any character whatsoever befell us en route, no dropping back into the basement with a low, grateful thud; no hitch; no delay of any kind. We were certainly out of luck that trip. The demon of a joyrider who operated the accursed device jerked a lever and up we soared at a distressingly high rate of speed. If I could have had my way about that youth he would have been arrested for speeding.

Now we were there! They rolled me into a large room, all white, with a rounded ceiling like the inside of an egg. Right away I knew what the feelings of a poor, lonely little yolk are when the spoon begins to chip the shell. If I had not been so busy feeling sorry for myself I think I might have developed quite an active sympathy for yolks.

My impression had been that this was to be in the nature of a private affair, without invitations. I was astonished to note that quite a crowd had assembled for the opening exercises. From his attire and general deportment I judged that Doctor

Z was going to be the master of the revels,
he being attired appropriately in a white
domino, with rubber gloves and a fancy
cap of crash toweling. There were present,
also, my diagnostic friend, Doctor X, likewise in fancy-dress costume, and a surgeon
I had never met. From what I could
gather he was going over the course behind
Doctor Z to replace the divots.

And there was an interne in the back-
ground, playing caddy, as it were, and a
head nurse, who was going to keep the
score, and two other nurses, who were going
to help her keep it. I only hoped that
they would show no partiality, but be as
fair to me as they were to Doctor Z, and
that he would go round in par.

So they placed me right where my eyes
might rest on a large wall cabinet full of
very shiny-looking tools; and they took my
cigar away from me and folded my hands
on the wide bowknot of my sash. Then
they put a cloth dingus over my face and
a voice of authority told me to breathe.
That advice, however, was superfluous and
might just as well have been omitted, for

such was my purpose anyhow. Ever since I can recall anything at all, breathing has been a regular habit with me. So I breathed. And, at that, a bottle of highly charged sarsaparilla exploded somewhere in the immediate vicinity and most of its contents went up my nose.

I started to tell them that somebody had been fooling with their ether and adulterating it, and that if they thought they could send me off to sleep with soda pop they were making the mistake of their lives, because it just naturally could not be done; but for some reason or other I decided to put off speaking about the matter for a few minutes. I breathed again—again—agai——

I was going away from there. I was in a large gas balloon, soaring up into the clouds. How pleasant! . . . No, by Jove! I was not in a balloon—I myself was the balloon, which was not quite so pleasant. Besides, Doctor Z was going along as a passenger; and as we traveled up and up he kept jabbing me in the midriff with the ferrule of a large umbrella which he had

brought along with him in case of rain.
He jabbed me harder and harder. I re-
monstrated with him. I told him I was a
bit tender in that locality and the ferrule of
his umbrella was sharp. He would not
listen. He kept on jabbing me. . . .

Something broke! We started back down
to earth. We fell faster and faster. We
fell nine miles, and after that I began to
get used to it. Then I saw the earth be-
neath and it was rising up to meet us.

A town was below—a town that grew
larger and larger as we neared it. I could
make out the bonded indebtedness, and the
Carnegie Library, and the moving-picture
palaces, and the new dancing parlor, and
other principal points of interest.

At the rate we were falling we were certainly going to make an awful splatter in
that town when we hit. I was sorry for the
street-cleaning department.

We fell another half mile or so. A spire
was sticking up into the sky directly be-
neath us, like a spear, to impale us. By a
supreme effort I twisted out of the way of
that spire, only to strike squarely on top of

the roof of a greenhouse back of the parsonage, next door. We crashed through it with a perfectly terrific clatter of breaking glass and landed in a bed of white flowers, all soft and downy, like feathers.

And then Doctor Z stood up and combed the débris out of his whiskers and remarked that, taking it by and large, it had been one of the pleasantest little outings he had enjoyed in the entire course of his practice. He said that as a patient I was fair, but as a balloon I was immense. He asked me whether I had seen anything of his umbrella and began looking round for it. I tried to help him look, but I was too tired to exert myself much. I told him I believed I would take a little nap.

I opened a dizzy eye part way. So this was heaven—this white expanse that swung and swam before my languid gaze? No, it could not be—it did not smell like heaven. It smelled like a hospital. It was a hospital. It was my hospital. My nurse was bending over me and I caught a faint whiff of the starch in the front of her crisp blue blouse. She was two-headed for the moment, but that was a mere detail. She settled a pillow under my head and told me to lie quiet.

I meant to lie quiet; I did not have to be told. I wanted to lie quiet and hurt. I was hurty from head to toe and back again, and crosswise and cater-cornered. I hurt diagonally and lengthwise and on the bias. I had a taste in my mouth like a bird-and-animal store. And empty! It seemed to me those doctors had not left anything inside of me except the acoustics. Well, there was a mite of consolation there. If the overhauling had been as thorough as I had reason to believe it was from my present sensations, I need never fear catching anything again so long as I lived, except possibly dandruff.

I waved the nurse away. I craved solitude. I desired only to lie there in that bed and hurt—which I did.

I had said beforehand I meant to stay in St. Germicide's for two or three days only. It is when I look back on that resolution I emit the hollow laugh elsewhere referred to. For exactly four weeks I was flat on

[47]

my back. I know now how excessively
wearied a man can get of his own back,
how tired of it, how bored with it! And
after that another two weeks elapsed before
my legs became the same dependable pair
of legs I had known in the past.

I did not want to eat at first, and when
I did begin to want to they would not let
me. If I felt sort of peckish they let me
suck a little glass thermometer, but there
is not much nourishment really in ther-
mometers. And for entertainment, to while
the dragging hours away, I could count the
cracks in the ceiling and read my temperature chart, which was a good deal like Red
Ames' batting average for the past season
—ranging from ninety-nine to one hundred
and four.

Also, through daily conversations with
my nurse and with the surgeons who
dropped in from time to time to have a
look at me, I learned, as I lay there, a great
deal about the medical profession—that is,
a great deal for a layman—and what I
learned filled me with an abiding admira-
tion for it, both as a science and as a busi-

ness. This surely is one profession which ever keeps its face to the front. Burying its past mistakes and forgetting them as speedily as possible, it pushes straight forward into fresh fields and fresh patients, always hopeful of what the future may bring in the way of newly discovered and highly expensive ailments. As we look backward upon the centuries we are astonished by its advancement. I did a good deal of looking backwards upon the centuries during my sojourn at St. Germicide's.

Take the Middle Ages now—the period when a barber and a surgeon were one and the same. If a man made a failure as a barber he turned his talents to surgery. Surgeons in those times were a husky breed. I judge they worked by the day instead of by piecework; anyhow the records show they were very fond of experiments, where somebody else furnished the raw material.

When there came a resounding knock at the tradesman's entrance of the moated grange, the lord of the manor, looking over the portcullis and seeing a lusty wight standing down below, in a leather apron, with his sleeves rolled up and a kit of soldering tools under his arm, didn't know until he made inquiry whether the gentle stranger had come to mend the drain or remove the cook's leg.

A little later along, when gunpowder had come into general use as a humanizing factor of civilization, surgeons treated a gunshot wound by pouring boiling lard into it, which I would say was calculated to take the victim's mind off his wound and give him something else to think about—for the time being, anyhow. I assume the notion of applying a mustard plaster outside one's stomach when one has a pain inside one's stomach is based on the same principle.

However, one doesn't have to go clear back to medieval times to note the radical differences in the plan of treating human ailments. A great many persons who are still living can remember when the doctors were not nearly so numerous as they are now. I, for one, would be the last to reverse the sentence and say that because the

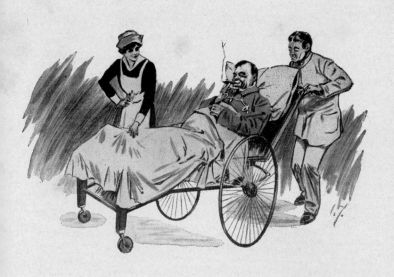

I WISHED TO SHOW
HOW UTTERLY INDIFFERENT I WAS

doctors were not nearly so numerous then as they are now, those persons are still living so numerously.

In the spring of the year, when the sap flowed and the birds mated, the sturdy farmer felt that he was due to have something the matter with him, too. So he would ride into the country-seat and get an almanac. Doubtless the reader, if country raised, has seen copies of this popular work. On the outside cover, which was dark blue in color, there was a picture of a person whose stomach was sliced four ways, like a twenty-cent pie, and then folded back neatly, thus exposing his entire interior arrangements to the gaze of the casual observer. However, this party, judging by his picture, did not appear to be suffering. He did not even seem to fear that he might catch cold from standing there in his own draught. He was gazing off into space in an absent-minded kind of way, apparently not aware that anything was wrong with him; and on all sides he was surrounded by interesting exhibits, such as a crab, and a scorpion, and a goat, and a chap with a bow and arrow—and one thing and another.

Such was the main design of the cover, while the contents were made up of recognized and standard varieties in the line of jokes and the line of diseases which alternated, with first a favorite joke and then a favorite disease. The author who wrote the descriptions of the diseases was one of the most convincing writers that ever lived anywhere. As a realist he had no superiors among those using our language as a vehicle for the expression of thought. He was a wonder. If a person wasn't particular about what ailed him he could read any page at random and have one specific disease. Or he could read the whole book through and have them all, in their most advanced stages. Then the only thing that could save him was a large dollar bottle.

Again, in attacks of the breakbone ague or malaria it was customary to call in a local practitioner, generally an elderly lady of the neighborhood, who had none of these latter-day prejudices regarding the use of tobacco by the gentler sex. One whom I distantly recall, among childhood's happy memories, carried this liberal-mindedness to a point where she not only dipped snuff and smoked a cob pipe, but sometimes chewed a little natural leaf. This lady, on being called in, would brew up a large caldron of medicinal roots and barks and sprouts and things; and then she would deluge the interior of the sufferer with a large gourdful of this pleasing mixture at regular intervals. It was efficacious, too. The inundated person either got well or else he drowned from the inside. Rocking the patient was almost as dangerous a pastime as rocking the boat. This also helps to explain, I think, why so many of our forebears had floating kidneys. There was nothing else for a kidney to do.

By the time I attained to long trousers, people in our town mainly had outgrown the unlicensed expert and were depending more and more upon the old-fashioned family doctor—the one with the whisker-jungle—who drove about in a gig, accompanied by a haunting aroma of iodoform and carrying his calomel with him in bulk.

He probably owned a secret calomel mine of his own. He must have; otherwise he could never have afforded to be so generous with it. He also had other medicines with him, all of them being selected on the principle that unless a drug tasted like the very dickens it couldn't possibly do you any good. At all hours of the day and night he was to be seen going to and fro, distributing nuggets from his private lode. He went to bed with his trousers and his hat on, I think, and there was a general belief that his old mare slept between the shafts of the gig, with the bridle shoved up on her forehead.

It has been only a few years since the oldtime general practitioner was everywhere. Just look round and see now how the system has changed! If your liver begins to misconduct itself the first thought of the modern operator is to cut it out and hide it some place where you can't find it. The oldtimer would have bombarded it with a large brunette pill about the size and color of a damson plum. Or he might put you on a diet of molasses seasoned to taste with blue mass and quinine and other attractive condiments. Likewise, in the spring of the year he frequently anointed the young of the species with a mixture of mutton suet and asafetida. This treatment had an effect that was distinctly depressing upon the growing boy. It militated against his popularity. It forced him to seek his pleasures outdoors, and a good distance outdoors at that.

It was very hard for a boy, however naturally attractive he might be, to retain his popularity at the fireside circle when coated with mutton suet and asafetida and then taken into a warm room. He attracted attention which he did not court and which was distasteful to him. Keeping quiet did not seem to help him any. Even if they had been blindfolded others would still have felt his presence. A civit-cat suffers from the same drawbacks in a social way, but the advantage to the civit-cat is that as a general thing it associates only with other civit-cats.

Except in the country the old-time, catch-as-catch-can general practitioner appears to be dying out. In the city one finds him occasionally, playing a limit game in an office on a back street—two dollars to come in, five to call; but the tendency of the day is toward specialists. Hence the expert who treats you for just one particular thing. With a pain in your chest, say, you go to a chest specialist. So long as he can keep the trouble confined to your chest, all well and good. If it slips down or slides up he tries to coax it back to the reservation. If it refuses to do so, he bids it an affectionate adieu, makes a dotted mark on you to show where he left off, collects his bill and regretfully turns you over to a stomach specialist or a throat specialist, depending on the direction in which the trouble was headed when last seen.

Or, perhaps the specialist to whom you take your custom is an advocate of an immediate operation for such cases as yours and all others. I may be unduly sensitive on account of having recently emerged from the surgeon's hands, but it strikes me now that there are an awful lot of doctors who take one brief glance at a person who is complaining, and say to themselves that here is something that ought to be looked into right away—and immediately open a bag and start picking out the proper utensils. You go into a doctor's office and tell him you do not feel the best in the world—and he gives you a look and excuses himself, and steps into the next room and begins greasing a saw.

Mind you, in these casual observations as compiled by me while bedfast and here given utterance, I am not seeking to disparage possibly the noblest of professions. Lately I have owed much to it. I am strictly on the doctor's side. He is with us when we come into the world and with us when we go out of it, oftentimes lending a helping hand on both occasions. Anyway, our sympathies should especially go out to the medical profession at this particular time when the anti-vivisectionists are railing so loudly against the doctors. The anti-vivisection crusade has enlisted widely different classes in the community, including many lovers of our dumb-animal pets— and aren't some of them the dumbest things you ever saw!—especially chow dogs and love birds.

I will admit there is something to be said on both sides of the argument. This dissecting of live subjects may have been carried to extremes on occasions. When I read in the medical journals that the eminent Doctor Somebody succeeded in transferring the interior department of a pelican to a pointer pup, and vice versa, with such success that the pup drowned while diving for minnows, and the pelican went out in the back yard and barked himself to death baying at the moon, I am interested naturally; but, possibly because of my ignorance, I fail to see wherein the treatment of infantile paralysis has been materially advanced. On the other hand, I would rather the kind and gentle Belgian hare should be offered up as a sacrifice upon the operating table and leave behind him a large family of little Belgian heirs and heiresses—dependent upon the charity of a cruel world—than that I should have something painful which can be avoided through making him a martyr. I would rather any white rabbit on earth should have the Asiatic cholera twice than that I should have it just once. These are my sincere convictions, and I will not attempt to disguise them.

Thanks, too, to medical science we know about germs and serums and diets and all that. Our less fortunate ancestors didn't know about them. They were befogged in ignorance. As recently as the generation immediately preceding ours people were unacquainted with the simplest rules of hygiene. They didn't care whether the housefly wiped his feet before he came into the house or not. The gentleman with the drooping, cream-separator mustache was at perfect liberty to use the common drinking cup on the railroad train. The appendix lurked in its snug retreat, undisturbed by the prying fingers of curiosity. The fever-bearing skeeter buzzed and flitted, stinging where he pleased. The germ theory was unfathomed. Suitable food for an invalid was anything the invalid could afford to buy. Fresh air, and more especially fresh night air, was regarded as dangerous, and people hermetically sealed themselves in before retiring. Not daily as at present was the world gladdened by the tidings that science had un-

earthed some new and particularly unpleas-
ant disease. It never occurred to a mother
that she should sterilize the slipper before
spanking her offspring. Babies were not
reared antiseptically, but just so. Nobody
was aware of microbes.

In short, our sires and our grandsires
abode in the midst of perils. They were
surrounded on all sides by things that are
immediately fatal to the human system.
Not a single one of them had a right to
pass his second birthday. In the light of
what we know, we realize that by now this
world should be but a barren waste, dotted
at frequent intervals with large graveyards
and populated only by a few dispossessed
and hungry bacteria, hanging over the
cemetery fence singing: Driven From
Home!

In the conditions generally prevalent up
to twenty-five years ago, most of us never
had any license, really, to be born at all.
Yet look how many of us are now here.
In this age of research I hesitate to attempt
to account for it, except on the entirely un-
scientific theory that what you don't know
doesn't hurt you. Doubtless a physician

could give you a better explanation, but his would cost you more than mine has.

But we digress. Let us get back to our main subject, which is myself. I shall never forget my first real meal in that hospital. There was quite a good deal of talk about it beforehand. My nurse kept telling me that on the next day the doctor had promised I might have something to eat. I could hardly wait. I had visions of a tenderloin steak smothered in fried onions, and some French-fried potatoes, and a tall table-limit stack of wheat cakes, and a few other incidental comfits and kickshaws. I could hardly wait for that meal.

The next day came and she brought it to me, and I partook thereof. It was the white of an egg. For dessert I licked a stamp; but this I did clandestinely and by stealth, without saying anything about it to her. I was not supposed to have any sweets.

On the occasion of the next feast the diet was varied. I had a sip of one of those fermented milk products. You probably know the sort of thing I mean. Even before you've swallowed it, it tastes as though

it had already disagreed with you. The
nurse said this food was predigested but
did not tell me by whom. Nor did I ask
her. I started to, but thought better of it.
Sometimes one is all the happier for not
knowing too much.

A little later on, seeing that I had not
suffered an attack of indigestion from this
debauch, they gave me junket. In the dictionary I have looked up the definitions of
junket. I quote:

JUNKET, *v.* I. *t.* To entertain by feasting;
regale. II. *i.* To give or take part in an
entertainment or excursion; feast in company; picnic; revel.

JUNKET, *n.* A merry feast or excursion;
picnic.

When the author of a dictionary tries to
be frivolous he only succeeds in making
himself appear foolish.

I know not how it may be in the world
at large, but in a hospital, junket is a custard that by some subtle process has been
denuded of those ingredients which make
a custard fascinating and exciting. It tastes
as though the eggs, which form its under-

lying basis, had been laid in a fit of pique by a hen that was severely upset at the time.

Hereafter when the junket is passed round somebody else may have my share. I'll stick to the mince pie *à la mode*.

And the first cigar of my convalescence —ah, that, too, abides as a vivid memory! Dropping in one morning to replace the wrappings Doctor Z said I might smoke in moderation. So the nurse brought me a cigar, and I lit it and took one deep puff; but only one. I laid it aside. I said to the nurse:

"A mistake has been made here. I do not want a cooking cigar, you understand. I desire a cigar for personal use. This one is full of herbs and simples, I think. It suggests a New England boiled dinner, and not a very good New England boiled dinner at that. Let us try again."

She brought another cigar. It was not satisfactory either. Then she showed me the box—an orthodox box containing cigars of a recognized and previously dependable brand. I could only conclude that a root-and-herb doctor had bought an interest in the business and was introducing his own pet notions into the formula.

"Speaking of Operations—"

But came a day—as the fancy writers say when they wish to convey the impression that a day has come, but hate to do it in a commonplace manner—came a day when my cigar tasted as a cigar should taste and food had the proper relish to it; and my appetite came back again and found the old home place not so greatly changed after all.

And then shortly thereafter came another day, when I, all replete with expensive stitches, might drape the customary habiliments of civilization about my attenuated frame and go forth to mingle with my fellow beings. I have been mingling pretty steadily ever since, for now I have something to talk about—a topic good for any company; congenial, an absorbing topic.

I can spot a brother member a block away. I hasten up to him and give him the grand hailing sign of the order. He opens his mouth to speak, but I beat him to it.

"Speaking of operations ——" I say. And then I'm off.

Believe me, it's the life!

stitches, might drape the customary habiliments of civilization about my attenuated